A Bear's Tale: Stories of My Life

By

Alexander T. Bear

as told to Susan Eileen Walker

A Coop McK, LLC Publication

Title: A Bear's Tale: Stories of My Life
Copyright © 2016 Susan Eileen Walker

Cover design by: Jinger Bruton

Printed in the United States of America

First Printing,   2016

ISBN: 978-9-988-5237-6-0

Dedication

To Teddy Bear Lovers everywhere and military families
whose sacrifices keep us safe.

1917: The First Christmas

I suppose I should start at the beginning. Edward Quigglebush rescued me from a little shop in France. It was 1917, and a war was raging.

There was not much else in the shop, just some other animals and dolls and toys. The shop had sold all its food, and other things people needed. In fact, the owner had left us behind and moved to England. Six children moved in two days later. They tried to sell the toys, but no one wanted toys. People wanted food and shoes and clothes and gasoline, not stuffed bears or china dolls.

The day before Christmas, the younger children were complaining about being hungry and the older ones were talking about how to earn enough money to buy dinner. They didn't think about Christmas or presents or turkey or ham or candy. They just wanted some bread and cheese to keep away the hunger.

Edward came in about that time. "What do you have for the girl who is going to be my wife?" All the children stopped talking and stared at him.

The oldest girl, Anna, stepped forward. "We have dolls and stuffed animals, a few games. All good toys a young woman might like," she said in English.

The soldier looked at the dolls, but they were fragile and frilly. His Mary wasn't like that. Mary was soft and sweet, and he loved her.

He stopped at the shelf where I sat with a family of monkeys and some other bears. He picked us up one by one. He stared at me and I stared back at him, my black button eyes not able to blink. He put me down, and I was sure I wouldn't be going with him to meet the girl he was going to marry. After he tested the others, he picked me up again.

He looked at the tag tied on my arm. "Alexander, eh? Well, you look like the perfect bear to watch over my Mary when I can't," Edward said.

"Ah, a beautiful bear for a beautiful girl," Anna said.

Edward looked at the rest of the empty room. "Yes, I'll take this one."

Anna nodded and said, "Twenty francs, please," in her most adult voice.

The other children broke into excited whispers as Edward dug into his pocket. Twenty francs would buy bread and cheese and even a treat, if they could find one for sale.

Edward counted out the twenty francs, then added another ten. "There's a place not too far from here that's taking care of orphans. They have beds and blankets, and hot food. There are lots of other children to play with."

"Merci, monsieur, but we'll be fine here. Happy Christmas," Anna said with a smile.

Edward and I left the shop and returned to the hospital where he and his future wife, Mary, worked. He pulled a shiny yellow ring out of one pocket, and a frilly pink ribbon out of another. "Now, look here, Mr. Bear," he said, "don't you lose this ring. I've carried it for a long time, waiting for just the right moment to ask Mary to be my wife."

I wanted to squirm under the sissy pink ribbon, but I could not move. So I wore pink until we met Mary on the roof of the hospital just before midnight. The sky was clear, with a whole lot of stars shining brightly. It was cold, but they didn't seem to care. I'm a bear. I have fur so cold doesn't bother me too much.

Edward hid me behind his back until Mary was right in front of him. Then he pulled me out and held me up for Mary to see.

"Merry Christmas, Mary. Will you be my wife?"

Mary laughed at his words. She looked at Edward, then looked at me again. "Be your wife?"

"Marry me and be my wife," Edward insisted.

"I'd be honored," she replied.

Edward untied that silly pink ribbon from around my neck and slid the ring on Mary's finger.

"This is Alexander T. Bear. He's going to keep us safe, forever," he introduced me. I would have bowed, but bears do not bend in the middle on their own.

That's when the church bells began to ring. It was midnight on Christmas Day, 1917, and I had just become the protector bear for Edward and Mary and all the Quigglebushes to come.

1920: Thanksgiving, No Turkey?

Back in 1920 when I was just a cub, Mary and I were living with her family in Tennessee. Edward was away with the Army. I was there to protect Mary while she waited for her baby to arrive. I also protected her mama and papa and all her brothers and sisters.

Mary's folks were farmers. They grew the vegetables and fruits they ate. They also raised cows for milk, chickens for eggs, and pigs for meat. For Thanksgiving, they wanted something special, a turkey. People didn't run to the grocery store to buy food like they do nowadays.

For a Thanksgiving turkey, the men had to go hunting. Every day for a week Mary's papa and brothers went into the mountains behind the farm. But they never found a turkey. There had been a fire up in the mountains that summer, and all the animals had moved away.

"There's not a turkey in the county to be had. I guess we'll just have to make do without one this year," Mary's papa said, the day before Thanksgiving.

"It's all right. We'll still have potatoes, and corn pudding, and pickles, and beans. I'll make pie for dessert," Mary's mama said, trying to be cheerful.

Mary didn't say anything. The house was small, so I could hear everything that was said even if I wasn't in the room. She just excused herself and came to the room we shared at the back of the house.

"It won't be the same without a turkey, Alexander," she told me quietly. "There must be something I can do."

I wanted to tell her there wasn't anything she could do except have her baby, but she left the room before I could figure out that three-year-old stuffed bears really can't give advice since they can't talk.

Mary and her sisters came back carrying a pumpkin and a sack full of dried cornhusks. Then they left again. When they returned, they had a squash, a carrot and their mama's sewing kit. Then they went to work.

I couldn't see exactly what they were doing, but those girls whispered and giggled and worked the rest of the afternoon. When they were done, Mary draped a towel over whatever it was so no one could see it, not even me. I thought that was rude. If it was a secret, I wouldn't tell.

The next day, Thanksgiving, Mary's youngest sister, Sarah, brought me out to the dining room to be with the rest of the family. I sat on the sideboard next to the apple pie. That way I could see, but was out of danger of being dunked in the gravy.

Just before dinner was served, Mary cleared a space in the middle of the table, then disappeared into her room. She returned carrying the tray with the towel over it. She set the tray in the space in the middle of the table, then carefully lifted the towel off her creation.

"A turkey!" Mary's mama said.

"Sure enough," her father agreed.

The girls had made their turkey using the pumpkin as the plump body, the cornhusks as the tail feathers, and the squash and carrot as the head, neck, and beak.

"Just because we can't eat turkey, doesn't mean that we can't look at one," Sarah said.

"It's perfect," her mother said, as she placed the last of their dinner on the table.

Three days later, Mary had her baby, Michael, in her little room at the back of the house. I was right there beside her the whole time, keeping her safe.

1925: Runaways and Pirates

In 1925, we were stationed at Fort William D. Davis in the Canal Zone of Panama. That's the big ditch someone dug across the country separating North America from South America. The Army's 14th Infantry had protected the Panama Canal since it had opened in 1917 while we were in France.

Michael was five years old and had a brand new baby brother named Sam. He wasn't happy about Sam. He didn't like to share his mama. I didn't blame him, but Sam was now a member of the family. We had to love him no matter how much noise he made.

One day while we were supposed to be taking a nap, Michael whispered to me, "Mama's too busy with Sam. I'm running away. I'm going to the canal and become a pirate and sail all over the world. You're coming, too. We'll leave tomorrow."

I didn't think we should run away. Neither one of us spoke Spanish. I didn't want to be a pirate. Pirates were ugly with eye patches and wooden legs. They wore funny clothes and said "Har! Har! Har!" when they laughed. I didn't think I could laugh like that. Besides, I just knew pirates didn't get to play all day like we did.

The next morning, Michael came into the living room carrying the large basket his mother took to the market every few days. He had some of his clothes and toys packed in the bottom.

"Come on, Alexander. We're going to run away and become pirates. No one here will miss us." Michael picked me up and laid me on top of the basket, making sure I didn't fall out.

"Bye, Mama," he called, as we walked out the front door. She didn't answer. Sam was crying again.

On the porch, Michael passed Maria who cleaned the house and cooked the food. "Buenos dias, Maria," he called, as he stomped down the steps.

"Buenos dias, Senor Miguel. Off to play?"

"Yes." Michael didn't stop to chat. We were off to become pirates.

"Don't go too far," Maria called, before returning to her sweeping.

Michael waved over his shoulder as he left the yard. He turned right at the side of the road. "The canal must be this way. This is how Daddy goes to work each morning."

Michael didn't stop until we were at the edge of town. Our house was way out of sight. The road split in two and both roads headed into the jungle.

"Which way?" Michael stopped for a moment, setting the basket in the dirt. Why was he asking me? I didn't have a map.

He studied both roads, finally deciding on the left one. Michael walked and walked and walked. The road twisted and turned, but we never found the canal. When we came to the next place where the road divided into two, Michael decided to take the right road. I still didn't see any boats, and I didn't think we would ever get to the canal.

It began to rain. The rain got real hard; we could hardly see anything around us. In minutes we were both soaked and the dirt road around us was all muddy. Then the rain stopped as suddenly as it had begun.

"I'm cold and I'm getting hungry. Maybe being a pirate wasn't such a good idea. I want to go home. I wish Mama was here." Michael hugged me tight.

Turning back, Michael held me under one arm and carried the basket in his other hand. He sloshed through the mud, careful to hold the basket high enough so it wouldn't drag in the mud.

A few minutes later, he stopped and turned around. Something that sounded like thunder was roaring down the road behind us. Was the storm coming back? If it started to rain again, I was sure we would drown in the mud. The thunder got louder and louder.

Suddenly horses came around the bend, heading straight at us. We were going to be run over by a bunch of big, smelly horses!

I was ready to move out of the way and let those smelly beasts go by. Then once they were gone, Michael could take us back home again. Except Michael didn't move. He just stood there, frozen, staring at the horses.

One horse broke away and came ahead of the others. A soldier was riding that one. He wore the tan uniform all the Army soldiers wore, but looked more like a cowboy than a soldier on his horse.

He raced to us, bending way over as he did. I thought he was going to fall off and get trampled, but instead, he scooped Michael and me up with one arm.

His horse didn't even slow down as he lifted us off the road and set us in the saddle in front of him. Michael held me so tight I was afraid he would squeeze me in two.

No one spoke as we raced back through town. The other horses followed us all the way to the corral at the fort. The soldier guided his horse through the corral and out an opening on the other side. Another soldier closed that gate before the other horses could escape.

Only when the horses were inside the wooden fence and safe did the soldier finally speak. "What were you doing out in the middle of the jungle?"

He climbed down from the horse, then lifted us from the saddle. As soon as we were on the ground, Michael moved away from the horse.

"My mama loves Sam more than me so I was running away to the sea. I'm going to become a pirate." Michael gazed up at the soldier with wide, frightened eyes.

"Pirates aren't very nice people. Maybe you should stay here and become a Golden Dragon. The 14th Infantry is always looking for good soldiers."

"Can I join up now?" Michael asked.

I wasn't sure I wanted to be a horse soldier, but it had to be better than being a pirate. Whatever we did, I had to stay with Michael. It was my job to keep him safe, no matter what. So, if

Michael wanted to be around those horses, I guess we were going to be horse soldiers.

Michael didn't see his mom and dad behind him, but I did. His dad looked at the soldier and nodded. Then he turned and led Michael's mom away.

"What's your name, soldier?"

"Michael Quigglebush, sir."

"Well, Quigglebush, this is Scout and I'm Sergeant McKenna. The first thing a horse soldier does is take care of his mount."

We gave Scout a bath and brushed him dry. Then we cleaned his tack. I mostly watched but Michael cleaned and cleaned and cleaned.

After that, we made sure Scout had his lunch and plenty of water. Then it was time for Michael's lunch. Next, we carried vegetables from the fort's garden to the kitchen and wood from the huge woodpiles to the cook stoves. It was hard work. I could tell Michael was getting tired. Finally, Sergeant McKenna called for a break.

"I thought we'd be riding horses, and catching bad guys, and watching the canal for pirates. I feel more like a farmer than a soldier," Michael said. Then he took a drink of water the sergeant gave him.

"Sometimes we go for weeks without seeing any bad guys. Or rescuing people lost in the jungle. But we do these things every day, no matter what. We're just like a family. Everyone has to do his part."

Michael thought about that for a long time. "You know, I don't think I'm ready to be a horse soldier yet. If it's okay with you, I'll just go back to being a little boy."

Sergeant McKenna had a funny look on his face before asking, "Would you like a ride home?"

A couple of years later, Michael and I were again on the lookout for pirates. We were moving from Panama to California in 1928.

Michael and I were still best pals, so I didn't get boxed up with all his other toys. Instead, he carried me with him all the way. We rode on a big ship through the Panama Canal. The canal was actually cut through the mountains of Panama, dividing the country in half. We saw some pretty, colorful birds and even a couple of monkeys and alligators on that trip. After we left the canal, the ship chugged up the coast of Mexico to California.

Michael and I spent most of the trip keeping an eye out for pirates. One morning I was sure they'd found us. A large sailing ship came into view over the horizon. It was sailing toward us. It looked like they wanted to catch up with us.

"Look, Alexander, pirates!" Michael pointed.

I'd never seen pirates so I didn't know if that was a pirate ship or not.

He laid me across the railing to watch as the boat sailed closer. He ran to get an adult. Someone, anyone who would know what to do in case it really was pirates attacking the boat. He and his father got back just in time. I was getting ready to fall overboard. Thank goodness Michael pulled me back just before I fell into the ocean.

"There, Daddy! Pirates! Do you think they'll sink the ship?"

"I hope not. But we'd better keep an eye on them."

Michael and I spent the rest of the morning watching the boat as it sailed along, getting closer and closer. Finally it was right next to us. When the people on board called to the sailors on our boat, the sailors threw them a line, then sent a ladder down the side of the boat. Oh, no, the pirates were going to get us.

We watched, careful to stay well away from the pirates as they carried baskets of fruit up the ladder and onto the ship. But instead of kidnapping us, the pirates climbed back down the ladder and returned to their boat. It was all over in just a few minutes and then the pirates were sailing away again. We watched until it sailed out of sight.

"I guess they really weren't pirates, after all, Alexander. Maybe next time." Michael hugged me as the sailboat disappeared out of sight over the horizon.

1932: The President

In 1932, Mary, me, and the boys were visiting family in Washington, D. C. Since the boys were too big to be my pals any longer, Mary packed me in her suitcase. It was a tight fit, but at least I was with them.

Mary's niece, Ellen, saw me and we fell in love, so I didn't spend much time on the shelf in the guestroom. Instead, I got to tour the city with the rest of the family.

We saw the different monuments, but I thought the best part was visiting the President's house. He lives in a big house right in the middle of a big green yard. He even has gardens with lots of pretty flowers.

Now, I've been back to the White House since then. Things have changed a lot. A long time ago, visitors were not lead through the rooms on formal tours like they are these days. That started in 1961, I'm told.

Back when Ellen and I visited, people could pretty much wander through the public rooms at their own pace. Well, that's where we got into trouble.

Ellen got tired about halfway through looking at all the pretty rooms and furniture and things. When everyone else left the dining room, she and I stayed behind. It was a pretty room with a big sideboard cabinet along one wall.

Ellen crawled under the sideboard and pulled me under with her.

"I'm so tired, Alexander. Let's just rest here a while," she whispered.

I didn't argue, but I wasn't sure her mother would be real happy with us when we were found.

Ellen stretched out on the floor, holding me close to her chest and in just a few minutes, she was asleep.

I heard her mother calling and her sister whining about being tired and hungry, but I couldn't tell them where we were. Pretty soon their voices faded and they were gone, looking in the other rooms we'd been in.

Ellen didn't sleep long. When she woke up, we crawled back out from under the sideboard.

"Mama? Where are you?" she called, suddenly scared. We didn't hear or see anyone.

I wasn't scared, but I knew we'd be in trouble when we finally found her mother.

"Hello?" A man's voice called from the next room.

"Daddy?" Ellen ran toward the doorway, hoping her father had come to find her. But the man standing in the hallway wasn't her father. Ellen started to cry.

"Well, hello. Who are you?" The man knelt down in front of us.

"Ellen. Who are you?"

"My name's Mr. Hoover. Are you lost?"

"I'm not lost, I'm right here. My mama's lost. I stopped to rest and now everybody's gone." She began to cry harder.

"I was just going to get a cookie. Why don't you come with me and then we'll find your mama."

I wasn't going to argue. After all, he was a grown up.

Ellen stopped crying when he mentioned food. "Okay, Mr. Hoover. I like cookies."

"Me, too. Let's go." Mr. Hoover stood up, took Ellen's free hand and led the way to a big round room.

After sitting Ellen in a big rocking chair, he spoke softly to one of the ladies who sat outside the room. A few minutes later a man came in carrying a tray with two glasses of milk and a plate of cookies on it.

"These are sugar cookies. I hope you like them."

Ellen took a bite of her cookie and nodded. "They're very good."

Ellen and Mr. Hoover were talking about her favorite animals and toys when someone knocked on the door.

"I bet that's your mama," Mr. Hoover said with a smile. "Come in," he called to the door.

"Mama?" Ellen twisted in her seat while chewing a cookie.

"Ellen? Oh, Ellen what are you doing?"

"Me and Mr. Hoover's eating cookies," Ellen held up the proof. "They're really good."

Everyone had a cookie with Mr. Hoover. It wasn't until much later that Ellen and I understood that the nice man with the sugar cookies was the President of the United States.

1935: The Old Woman

On Independence Day, 1935, the town had a big picnic in the park. After playing hard with the big kids most of the afternoon, the newest Quigglebush family member, Sarah, and I stopped to rest on the family's picnic blanket. A little old lady sat down on the bench next to us. She had lots of wrinkles and pure white hair and walked with a cane

"Is that your special-secret sharing friend?" she asked Sarah.

"Yes, this is Alexander. He's been in our family since Daddy asked Mommy to marry him."

"I had a secret-sharing friend when I was your age," the lady said. "Her name was Lily." Then she told us about the trip she and her rag doll friend, Lily, took on the Underground Railroad.

Lily knew all my secrets, not that I had very many. My biggest secret was that I wanted to be free. Mama and Papa and I were slaves in North Carolina. Papa worked in the cotton fields, and Mama worked in the kitchen. I mostly stayed out of everyone's way. I played with Lily and the other slave children who were too young to work. Our mothers took turns keeping watch over us.

One night, Papa woke Lily and me up in the middle of the night. He hushed me when I started to complain.

"We're goin' North," he whispered. "You gotta keep still and silent or the men will catch us."

Mama helped me pull on both my dresses I had to wear. I wore one on top of the other that night. She handed me a heavy bundle.

"Don't lose this or we'll get mighty hungry on our trip," she said. "Don't say a word or we're sure to be caught. Then Master Edward will sell us away from here.

"I didn't want that to happen. I clenched my jaw to keep from asking the many questions I had and hugged Lily tight. Moments later, we slipped out of our little one-room house. Papa went first, then me, then Mama. We hid in the dark of the shadows, behind bushes and trees, careful not to make any noise.

"We moved slowly and quietly until we were far away. Papa chose our path and we walked and walked and walked. When I got tired, Papa carried me and Lily.

"When the sky began to get light, we found a big bush and hid underneath it. We covered ourselves with the leaves and pine needles and went to sleep. We walked two more nights like that before we met up with some other people. A lady led us, keeping to the streams and the woods, but always heading north. We hid when we heard people in the woods. We slept during the day, sometimes in a barn, but usually in the woods.

"Lily stayed with me the entire trip. I hugged her tight when I was too tired to walk farther, and I used her as a pillow when we slept during the day. She kept us safe during our trip north on the Underground Railroad.

"We didn't stop until we reached a small town way up in New York State. It was July 4, 1860. Papa went to work for a man who grew apples, and raised cows and horses. Mama cleaned the man's house and cooked for him. We lived in a three-room house, and he paid Papa and Mama to work for him.

"I still have Lily at home, even after seventy-five years. She's kept me company all my life, through life and death and illness. I still whisper my secrets to her sometimes, and she still keeps me safe."

1940: Bear-napped!

Being bear-napped is not a lot of fun. Especially when you get smooshed between a math book and a peanut butter sandwich. It happened in 1940 when Sarah took me to school. Her class was studying family history and traditions. I was her example of a family tradition.

"This is Alexander T. Bear," she said. "He's the good luck charm of our family."

She went on to explain how I had joined the family and kept everyone safe, in good times and bad. The class listened carefully and clapped when we were finished. Then we sat back down and another little girl got up to talk.

When everyone went outside to eat lunch and play, Sarah left me on her desk. We both figured I was safe there. I sat on her desk and studied the part of the room I could see. The room remained quiet until I heard a squeak behind me. Then someone slipped a cloth over my head.

Then the mystery person scooped me off Sarah's desk and stuffed me into a tight space that smelled like peanut butter and schoolbooks. A moment later, I was smooshed even more and everything went black.

I wanted to call out to Sarah to come rescue me, but being a stuffed bear, of course I couldn't. So I lay there with my face squished under me, hoping someone would put me back on Sarah's desk.

I thought the class was going to be outside forever. Finally they came in, talking and giggling, clumping around the wooden floor to their desks. That was when I was finally missed.

"Miss Moore, Alexander's gone!" I heard Sarah cry.

"Gone? How? He has to be around here somewhere," Miss Moore said.

"I left him right here on my desk and now he's gone. My mom and dad will never forgive me if I lost Alexander." I heard Sarah start to cry.

"Class, Alexander T. Bear is missing. If he is returned by the end of the day, there will be no questions asked. If not…" Miss Moore didn't finish her sentence. I thought I heard the whole class swallow.

The afternoon went on, with Miss Moore teaching science and English. I was still squeezed into a strange and most uncomfortable position. If I could move, I would have kicked until someone came to get me, but that wasn't possible.

"Now class, Alexander still hasn't been returned. We will sit here until the person who took him confesses and returns Sarah's bear," Miss Moore said in a stern voice at the end of the day. The room was so silent I thought I could hear Sarah sniffling nearby.

A moment later I was pulled out from my hiding place.

"I'm sorry, Sarah," a voice said as I changed hands. "I've never had a teddy bear, and he's so cute I just wanted to show my mom. I was going to bring him back tomorrow."

Now, I'm not cute, but she thought I was, so I didn't argue.

Somebody pulled the cloth from off my head, and then I was looking into Sarah's face. I wanted to hug her, but couldn't. Instead, I accepted the tight squeeze she gave me.

"All you had to do was ask," Sarah said. She turned me so I could see my bear-napper. I wanted to growl that stealing wasn't nice.

"All right, everyone, class dismissed," Miss Moore said from the front of the room. Everyone raced out, except Sarah and the bear-napper.

"Do you think I could borrow him? I'll bring him back tomorrow."

"I think it would be okay, but we'll have to ask my mom. Why don't you come home with me? You can carry him, if you want."

Sarah brushed my fur and handed me over.

The two girls walked home together. Sarah's mom said it was okay, so I got to spend the night with Sarah's new best friend. From then on, whenever I went to school for show and tell, I stayed on the teacher's desk where I was safe.

1944: The Blizzard

There was a time I wasn't sure New Year's would find us. How was I to know that New Year's wasn't like Santa Claus, the Easter Bunny or the Tooth Fairy? After all, time doesn't mean anything to me, a stuffed bear.

It was 1944 and Mike and I were traveling around northern Italy. Just two bachelors seeing the sites along with a bunch of other men during World War II.

Michael and I were given a Jeep and told to deliver a briefcase full of papers to the General. Mike's Captain gave us directions, but they were very confusing.We turned right at the first place where the road split and left at the second. When we got to the third, I couldn't remember where we were supposed to go. I don't think Mike did either. After all, he was the one who got us lost in Panama, remember?

As we were sitting there, trying to decide which way to drive, it began to snow. Mike turned to the right, hoping that was the correct road. In a few minutes, it was snowing so hard I could barely see the road. I don't know how Mike continued to drive, but he did.

We came to a town—or maybe it was just a wide spot in the road. Mike parked the Jeep and turned off the engine.

He stuck me inside his jacket, then picked up the briefcase of papers and the backpack that held everything we owned. He climbed from the Jeep and headed into the building right in front of us.

Once we were inside, I peeked out from Mike's coat. It was a barn. A small barn, but at least we were out of the snow. There were no animals and there was no food, but Mike's pack had food for a couple of days and at least the roof didn't leak.

"Well, Alexander. Looks like we're here for a while. I just hope no one decides to join us."

Mike wrapped his blanket around us, pulled hay on top of that so we were well insulated, and went to sleep. There wasn't much else he could do. We slept while the snow continued to fall and the wind kicked up. It snowed and snowed and snowed. Soon our Jeep was just a big lump in the snow near the barn.

When we woke up, we weren't alone in the barn. Someone was down on the main floor whispering. I didn't understand their words, but the voices sounded like children. I wanted to ask Mike if they let children fight in the war but, as usual, he didn't understand my stuffed bear questions.

He set me on top of his backpack, then slowly crawled to the edge of the loft and peeked over to the main floor. A moment later, he picked me up and climbed down the ladder.

Once we reached the main floor, I saw why he'd relaxed. The voices belonged to three small children who looked cold and hungry and sad. Mike spoke to them in English and then in another language I didn't understand. The oldest girl replied. I think they were as scared as we were.

The children had built a small fire with twigs and pieces of hay they'd collected. Mike broke up some of the loose boards and built up the fire. Soon the barn was toasty warm.

I felt kind of lost since I only spoke English. I know how to protect so I kept Mike and those kids safe. The littlest girl carried me everywhere with her and even slept beside me at night.

It was three days before the snow stopped falling. We were warm in the barn and Mike shared his food so no one got too hungry.

On the last morning together, the children woke us up with shouts of "Feliz nuovo anno." Mike told me they'd wished us Happy New Year in Italian. Outside the snow had stopped. Mike and the children unburied the Jeep while I guarded the barn. Then we all piled into the Jeep. The children pointed out the road to the town we were headed for. They climbed out at the next farmhouse down the road. Their parents greeted them with hugs, kisses—and scolding, I think.

The General was happy to see us, too, even if we were three days late.

1948: The Elephant

In 1948, Wayne took me to the noisiest, dirtiest, most incredible event I'd ever been to. It was a circus held under a tent in a great big field not too far from the base where we were stationed. Now, I'd been in tents before, but not one like this. It was HUGE! There were bleachers all around the outside of the tent and two circles in the middle.

Wayne and I sat in the third row of the bleachers with his dad, Michael. We were so close I ended up becoming part of the action.

"Look, Alexander, elephants!" Wayne held me over his head so I could see everything better.

The elephants were parading by, and one of them must have thought I was lunch. He turned his head, then reached out with his trunk and plucked me from Wayne's hands. I guess he thought I was a giant peanut.

"Hey, you, bring back my bear!" I heard Wayne yell over all the laughing and screaming and cries of surprise from the other children and adults in the crowd around him.

The elephant kept walking. He pulled his trunk in so he could taste me. I couldn't believe it. I wanted one of the people dancing around us to rescue me and return me to Wayne. But no one seemed to notice the bear. They rarely do.

The elephant licked me with his big, rough tongue. He must not have liked the way I tasted because he didn't eat me. Instead, he raised his trunk over his head and with a blaring snort, he tossed me away like I was trash.

I flew over two men who were throwing fiery sticks at one another, then hit the leg of a lady who was twirling around by her teeth. Then I fell down. But before I hit the ground to be trampled by a horse or that mean elephant, someone caught me.

I looked up into the strangest face I'd ever seen. It was all white with a purple nose and a rainbow for hair. He had orange lips and big red hearts where his eyes should be.

I want to go back to Wayne, I wanted to tell the creature. But he was laughing and holding me up and dancing around and around and around. The crowd laughed and giggled at his act until finally he danced out of the ring. Soon we were out of the light, and he tucked me under his arm and headed out of the tent.

"Well, little bear, thank you for helping out my act today, but I'm sure someone is missing you." The creature sounded like a man as we passed a group of dogs and two small horses. Was there a real person under that creature face? I wasn't sure I wanted to find out.

He carried me to a trailer that had a sign over the door: OFFICE. "You'll be safe here," said the creature. "Hopefully your friend will come and fetch you. If not, I may use you in my act every night. The kids really seemed to like it."

"Hey Dondo, who's your friend?" the lady in the office asked.

"I caught this guy in the middle of my act. I think Jumbo stole him from one of the kids in the audience."

"Alexander! You found my bear!" Wayne raced up, followed closely by his father.

Boy was I glad to see them. I didn't want to be a part of the circus. It was too noisy, smelly, and dangerous for a small bear. I'd rather have a hundred dangerous protector bear adventures instead.

1950: The Valentine

I'll bet you didn't know bears could fall in love. Well, we can! We just don't talk about it as well as people do. I remember the first time I fell in love.

It was 1951. Sam and I were working in a mobile hospital in Korea. We lived in a tent, and Sam worked at the hospital all the time. So we didn't get to have too many adventures together. That was okay with me. I'd found a girl to spend time with.

She was the most beautiful bear I'd ever seen. She was black and white and wore a fancy red ribbon around her neck. Now I've never liked to wear ribbons, but hers was beautiful.

Sam brought her to the tent we called home and set her next to me on the shelf he'd built for me. At first I wasn't sure I wanted to share my shelf, but who am I to complain? No one ever listens to a stuffed bear.

"Look Alex, I brought you a friend. Her name is Cleo. She can help you protect me. A least for a while," Sam said, as he set her down next to me.

Help me? I didn't need anyone's help in protecting Sam. He'd always been the easy one to keep safe. Not like his brother, Michael.

Sam turned us so we were facing each other. There was just enough room on the shelf so we didn't touch. Which was fine with me. Who wants to be holding paws with a stranger name Cleo?

That was before I got a good look at her. She was beautiful. So pretty and clean looking. I felt scruffy sitting next to her. There was only one thing that bothered me. She had two black eyes. I'd seen lots of black eyes when Sam and Michael were growing up, but theirs had always came from fighting. "So, did you win the fight where you got those black eyes?" I asked in my most polite bear whisper.

I thought she said something, but it didn't sound like words to me. At least not English words. I looked close, but she didn't answer me. She just stared at me with her big, black button eyes.

I stared back, with a warm fuzzy feeling in my chest that I'd never felt before. Cleo was beautiful, even if she wouldn't talk to me.

We sat for days that way. Not talking, not sharing the stories of our lives, just watching each other. The warm fuzzy feeling in my chest got bigger and bigger until I thought I would explode with it.

Every time the door opened, the shelf jumped a little bit and I slid closer and closer to Cleo. Finally, my paw touched hers. I thought it was wonderful even if I couldn't feel how soft her fur was.

One day Sam went and ruined it all. He came in with a box, packed her up and took her away. "Don't worry, old bear," he said to me, "I'm sending her to Jenny. You'll see her again as soon as

Jenny and I get married. Then you and Cleo can spend the rest of your lives keeping Jenny and me safe."

But I guess we just weren't meant to be together. Cleo never arrived at Jenny's house. I always thought she ended up with someone who needed her more than Jenny did. Someone who wasn't marrying into the Quigglebush family.

I didn't need her help protecting my family. But it had been fun having her around. Every time I think of her, I still get that warm fuzzy feeling in my chest.

1954: The Hurricane

In the fall of 1954, Sam and his bride, Jenny, had just been transferred to Fort Bragg, N.C. The job of keeping Sam safe had grown boring lately. That is, until Hurricane Hazel showed up.

Jenny and Sam often listened to the radio for weather reports. Jenny followed the neighbors' advice about getting ready for a hurricane. She collected candles, an oil lantern, and canned foods they could eat cold. She even packed a suitcase with clothes and supplies just in case we had to leave the house. I hoped they would remember the bear if they had to evacuate.

Hurricanes are famous for coming on shore at night. I don't know why, but they are. Hazel was different. She blew through in the middle of the day. No one expected that.

It was gray and cloudy that morning. The winds were gusty, but that wasn't unusual. It seemed the wind blew all the time lately. Sam had gone to work as usual and Jenny was cleaning house. Sam arrived home for lunch earlier than normal. He surprised us both.

"Hi," Jenny greeted him with a hug.

"You're not ready?" He glanced around the room. He looked worried.

"Ready for what?" Jenny asked.

"To evacuate. Everyone in this section of housing is to go to the auditorium until the storm passes. The hurricane changed directions and is coming this way. Grab the bag you packed. We've got to go now."

Jenny handed Sam the suitcase, then looked around the room. As newlyweds, they didn't have a lot, but she didn't want to lose anything. I wanted to call for her to take me with her. I didn't want to be left alone. They needed me to keep them safe.

"We can't leave Alexander. Your parents would never forgive us if we lost him!" Jenny said. She rushed across the living room and scooped me from the shelf where I lived.

Thank you. Jenny. I really didn't want to be left behind with the furniture.

Sam helped us into the car he'd borrowed, then drove across the base to the auditorium. No one else was driving on the road. The winds were growing stronger and the thunder rumbled across the sky. Just as Sam parked the car, it began to rain.

They ran to the large brick building, the wind pulling and pushing at them. I didn't get too wet, but they were soaked by the time we got inside.

A lady directed us into the main room of the building. It was dark in there. There were no windows and only a few lanterns around the room for light.

"Hey, Quigglebush, over here," someone called from the corner to the left.

Sam and Jenny and I joined their friends. They'd spread out two blankets on the floor and were sitting around like they were at a picnic. Mothers were holding children and everyone looked scared.

It was so quiet we could hear the storm outside. The wind howled. The thunder boomed. There were occasional thumps and bumps and crashes. Every time a loud noise sounded, Jenny jumped then hugged me closer.

The noise grew so loud I couldn't hear anything. Then the noise died away.

A voice boomed from the front of the room: "The storm isn't over. The eye is passing over us. The winds will start up again in a few minutes."

It wasn't long before the howling noise started again, louder than before. I was happy I was with Sam and Jenny and not back at the house all by myself.

Soon the winds died away and the thunder stopped rumbling. I wasn't sure whether the storm was over or if we'd been blown to Kansas like that girl Dorothy. The men went outside to check for damage. A lot of trees had fallen down. A couple of houses had blown away, but ours was still standing.

Hurricane Hazel was one of the most dangerous storms in history, but we'd survived it. The radio reported later she'd moved up the East Coast all the way to Canada, causing problems all along her path.

1959: Kissing a Cake

We were on the move again. It was 1959, and Molly and Jenny and I were traveling across the country. Sam had gone ahead to his new job in the hospital, but left me behind to keep his girls safe. He'd taken the car packed full of stuff, so we rode the train from Fort Bragg, North Carolina, to San Francisco, California.

Being only four years old, Molly was always finding adventures for us to get into. She couldn't just sit and watch the scenery flash by the wide train windows. Instead, we went exploring and I ended up in a pretty sticky situation.

When we stopped in Tennessee, a lady climbed on board our car. She sat down by herself and carefully placed a big round box covered in flowers in her lap. She held the box with both hands as if she were afraid it would disappear. Molly and I chatted with all the other people on the train. About dinnertime, we finally reached the lady with the box.

"Hi, I'm Molly and this is Alexander. What's your name?" Molly climbed into the seat next to the lady.

"Clara Brown," the lady answered softly.

"I'm going to San Francisco. Where are you going?" Molly asked.

"California. I'm going to get married to an Army soldier."

"Is that your dinner in the pretty box?" Molly asked, curious about the flower-covered round box on her lap.

"No, it's my wedding cake," Clara smiled as she answered.

The porter stepped into the train car and hurried to where we'd just gotten settled. "You'll have to move," he said.

"Why?" Molly asked.

"Not you, honey, her." The porter pointed at the lady next to us.

"Why?" Molly asked again.

"I have a ticket," Clara said. She pulled a piece of paper out of her pocket.

"Fine. But you'll have to move to the last car. That's the one for colored folk."

"Why?" Molly asked once again. It was her favorite word this week.

"Because that's just the way things are," the porter replied.

About that time, Jenny came up the aisle. "Is there a problem?"

"Yes, she needs to move to the last car," the porter pointed at Clara again.

"Mama, This is Clara Brown. She's going all the way to California to get married to a soldier, and she's got her wedding cake in the box. Can't she stay here with us?"

"I don't see why not. It's not like the train is very crowded," Jenny answered, staring down the porter.

"Are you willing to take responsibility for her?" the porter huffed.

"I'm sure she can be responsible for herself, but we'll be happy to travel with her if that would make you feel better," Jenny replied.

"Very well," the porter left. Jenny sat down in the seat facing Molly and Clara.

"Thank you." Clara said softly.

"I'm an Army wife myself," Jenny said. "You're marrying a soldier. It's time that the rest of the world treated everyone as equals. Is that really your wedding cake?" Jenny said.

"Yes. When Mama heard Joe and I were getting married as soon as I get there, she set about making us a cake. She wouldn't let me leave until she'd finished. 'Every bride deserves a proper wedding cake even if she can't have a proper wedding,' she said."

"Can I see it?" Molly asked.

"Yes." Clara smiled as she opened the box.

Molly leaned over and held me up so I could see, too. "Look Alexander. It's so pretty."

The cake was beautiful! White with fancy swirls and real daisies on top. But then Molly let go and I flew right into the middle of the box, landing face first on top of the cake.

"Oh, Alexander. What have you done?" Molly fussed. Clara picked me up and handed me back to the little girl. I had icing on my nose and some sugar in my eyebrows.

"Is the cake okay?" Molly sounded more worried about the cake than about me.

"It's fine, just a little dent where Mr. Alexander kissed the cake."

"Oh, that means you and the cake will get to California just fine. Alexander's our protector bear. If he kissed your cake that means he'll keep it safe, too."

And so I did. Molly and Jenny and Clara and I all got to California safe, with Jenny and Clara taking turns holding the wedding cake hatbox.

1964: The Closet Monster

Sometimes an active imagination can scare you more than your brother jumping out of a bush screaming at the top of his lungs. Danielle and I learned this in 1964.

Molly was spending the night with a friend. Sam and Jenny had gone out for the evening and left us with a babysitter. Normally I don't mind babysitters even though I'm not a baby, but this one seemed to be more interested in watching television than she was in taking care of us.

She put us to bed early and didn't even read us a bedtime story. When Danielle woke up from a dream, I did what I could, but she wanted someone to give her a hug. I couldn't do that.

We climbed out of bed and went to the living room. The babysitter was watching television with the lights off. Back then, television was black and white only. She looked funny in the flickering gray light.

I guess she scared Danielle, too. Instead of talking to the babysitter, she and I stayed in the hall and watched television for a few minutes. The show was about a hunt for a monster that liked to hide in dark closets. Finally, Danielle yawned and we went back to bed.

"It sure is dark, Alexander," she whispered in my ear. "I hope that monster doesn't come out of MY closet."

I wanted to tell her that monsters couldn't come out of closets if the door was closed. Her closet door was open partway. So then I wanted to tell her to go close the closet door. But I can't talk, so I could only accept the tight hug she gave me.

Danielle finally fell asleep, but tossed and turned and cried out softly a couple of times. I ended up being thrown on the floor where I could see under the bed, but not the closet door.

Nope, there were no monsters under the bed. But I wasn't so sure about the closet. And to make matters worse, Alexander, the family protector bear, couldn't see the closet door to do my job properly. That's when I heard Sam and Jenny come home.

A few minutes later Danielle cried out, "Mama!"

The hall light flicked on and then Jenny was there. She picked me up off the floor before kneeling beside the bed. "Danielle, what's wrong?" she asked, brushing Danielle's hair out of her face.

"There's a monster in my closet and he's gonna come out and eat me!" Danielle cried.

"A monster? Well, we'll just see about that." Jenny went to the closet and opened the door wide. Then she reached up and pulled a string. The light clicked on.

"There, see? No monster." She moved the clothes around on their hangers so Danielle could see. Just clothes and toys and shoes. It was a little messy, but no monsters.

"Okay, but close the door really hard. Then the monsters won't be able to come out."

Jenny pulled the cord and the light switched off. Then she shut the door tight. "Okay, now it's time for little girls and teddy bears to go to sleep."

Jenny handed me to Danielle, then tucked us both in and gave us each a kiss on our foreheads.

"Good night, sleep tight, don't let the bedbugs bite," Danielle and Jenny recited together as they did every night.

Then Danielle added, "Or monsters!"

After that, every night before she climbed into bed, Danielle made sure the closet door was closed all the way. And never again did the closet monsters bother us. But the under-the-bed monsters were another thing.

1967: The Balloon Ride

Having adventures with a friend is much more fun than having the adventure all alone. Maybe because with a friend along for the ride, you're not as scared as if you're alone. I found that out on a breezy spring day in 1967 when the entire family gathered for a celebration. Edward and Mary had been married for fifty years.

Anniversaries are the birthdays of a marriage. They come every year and some are much more special than others. Fifty is a really special anniversary. It's called the Golden Anniversary.

Well that day in May, the family gathered for a picnic in the park near Edward and Mary's house. I was living with Molly and Danielle, and their parents Sam and Jenny. Since I'd been such an important part of the family to that point, naturally I got to go to the party.

"Now, Alexander, I want you to hold onto these balloons and don't let them get away. Guard the cake and keep Danielle and Uncle Mike from eating it until the party," Molly said.

She'd tied several balloons to my arm before setting me on the table. I sat and watched the family and their friends gather for Edward and Mary's party. Just as the guests of honor arrived, a breeze started to blow.

The gold and white balloons I held shifted over my head. I felt the breeze ruffle my fur. I thought I moved away from the cake. I wanted to ask someone what was going on, but then it was too late! I was floating away!

"Molly, look! Alexander's flying!" Danielle called to her sister.

As I began rising from the table and floating across the grass, I saw the girls race toward me.

I was too high for them to reach me. Hey there, I wanted to call. Would someone please put the bear back on the table where he belongs?

"Daddy! Uncle Mike! Somebody! Alexander's flying away!" Molly and Danielle called to the crowd gathered around Edward and Mary.

Everyone turned to look where the girls were pointing. "Oh, no! Alexander, come down from there," Edward ordered as he led the grownups across the field. They chased me as I floated toward the trees and the river beyond.

Oh, no, not the river. Please don't let me fall into the water. Stuffed bears and water definitely are not a good combination, no matter what anyone says.

"How are we gonna get him down, Grampa?" Danielle asked as I drifted just out of reach of even the tallest adult.

"Get me a long stick, Dani," Michael ordered as he ran ahead of where I seemed to be heading. Right for the river.

Danielle and Molly ran back to where our picnic was laid out and searched for a long stick. The other men fanned out, looking as well. But there were no sticks around long enough to reach me. Sam picked up a small, sharp edged rock and threw it at me. It hit my chest and fell back to the ground. The next one flew higher and hit one of the balloons over my head.

Pop! I felt a jerk as one of the balloons popped. Then I began to slowly float downwards, landing in Mary's arms, two of my three balloons still intact.

"Oh, Alexander, what would we ever have done without you to protect us?" She hugged me tight, then untied the balloons from my arm. "I don't think we'll need these. You don't need any decorations to make you the most special bear in our lives." She handed the balloons to Danielle, who tied them to her own arm instead. They looked really good with her purple and white outfit.

Mary carried me back to my spot by the cake where I stayed until it was time to go home.

1971: The Monkeybird

In 1971, I learned what it was like to be a bird. It wasn't as much fun as I thought it should be.

"Hey, look at me!" Danielle called down, fearlessly clinging to the trunk of a tree. Personally, I thought we were too high, but then I never was too fond of being high without a plane around me.

All I could see around us were tree limbs and leaves. I couldn't even see the ground from where I was—sticking out of Danielle's backpack.

"Danielle, come down! You're too high," Jenny ordered from the ground.

Yeah, Danielle, let's get the bear out of the tree and back on the ground where it's safe.

"But Mom, I'm a monkey. Daddy always says so. And monkeys live in trees, so here I am. Look at me!"

"Come down, Danielle. You're too high and that tree is very old. It's not used to little girls climbing it." Jenny tried to keep the panic out of her voice when she looked up, up, up to see us in the old oak tree. We were so high she had to stand right next to the tree trunk to see exactly how high we were.

"All right, Mom," Danielle started to climb down.

We were almost to the ground, and I was starting to breathe again when her foot slipped off the branch just as she shifted her weight to it. We weren't too far from the ground, but we still made a loud thud when we landed. Thankfully, Danielle landed on one arm and not her backpack. Otherwise, this bear would have been a pancake.

"Ouch!" Danielle said as she sat up. Her arm was red, and she held it with her other hand.

"Are you okay?" Jenny asked, sitting down next to us. She brushed the grass out of Danielle's hair and off her shirt.

"My arm hurts," Danielle said. She pointed to just above her hand.

"Can you move your fingers?" Sam asked when he joined us under the old oak tree. He took her fingers and wiggled them, then tried to move her hand.

"Oww, that hurts!" Danielle couldn't help but cry. I wasn't feeling so good myself. After all, she climbed the tree because she wanted me to see a bird's nest she'd found the last time she'd climbed up there without her parents knowing about it.

"It's off to the doctor for you, Miss Monkeybird," Sam said, lifting us up and carrying us to the car.

"The doctor? Why?"

"I think you broke your wing," Sam said, as he put us in the car. "Monkey's aren't supposed to try to fly like birds."

We went to the hospital and Danielle had pictures taken of her arm. They were pictures that showed the inside part of her arm.

The doctor pointed to a place just above the wrist. "It's cracked right here," he said.

"What are you going to do now?" Danielle asked. She wasn't sure about any of this. Neither was I, but doctors are supposed to help people, not hurt them more, so we waited for his answer.

"Well, Miss Monkeybird, we are going to put that wing in a cast for a month so that it has a chance to heal. And I'd advise not trying to fly again." The doctor smiled as he reached for some special cast materials.

"Can Alexander have a cast too?" Danielle asked. I didn't think I needed one. After all, I'm a bear and I didn't break MY arm.

"We'll gave Alexander a special cast that won't mess up his fur. That way you'll see that getting a cast won't hurt," the doctor said.

Danielle held me in her arm while the doctor put a cast on me, explaining what he was doing every step of the way. When it came to her turn, Sam held Danielle on his lap, and the doctor carefully wrapped her arm in the cast.

For the next month, Danielle and I wore our casts and tried not to complain too much about the itching or the fact that it was hard to do some things. Danielle also learned to be more careful when she climbed trees.

1974: The Imposter

In 1974, I decided I should have been twins or maybe even triplets. The family was growing, and this one bear was having a tough time keeping up with all the protecting that needed to be done. It meant lots of adventures and not too much time sitting on a shelf somewhere dreaming of the past.

Karen had just turned three and was starting to be fun to play with. She finally decided I was pretty cool so she carried me with her everywhere. We'd become best buddies when the family told her she had to give me up. They told her it was because I needed to protect the newest addition to the Quigglebush's extended family who was due to arrive at any minute.

Well, Karen didn't like that. She wrapped both arms around my middle and shook her head. She said simply, "No, Alex mine!" then stuck her bottom lip out and pouted.

I could tell the bear was going to get hurt if anyone tried to take me away from her. Thank goodness no one tried. I don't like being in the middle of fights, and Karen was determined to keep me.

"I had a feeling this was going to be a problem," Karen's great-grampa, Edward, said. "We should have bought you boys each your own protector bear. Then your mother and I would still have Alexander protecting us and you'd have bears of your own to worry with."

But then the bear would be sitting on a shelf somewhere, bored and dusty instead of having adventures and seeing the world. Thank goodness they'd let me be the only bear in the family.

"So, what do we do now?" Mike asked. As her grandfather, Mike refused to do anything to make Karen cry. To him, it was the saddest sound in the world.

"I'd say it's time to buy Alexander a helper, or maybe four or five," Edward suggested.

A helper? I don't need anyone's help. This family just needed to stop growing so fast. But no one listens to the bear.

A week later, baby Josh came home from the hospital and the family gathered to welcome him. Sam, the brand new grampa, showed up with a bear under his arm that looked an awful lot like another bear we all know and love.

Karen and I studied this newcomer. He was brown and furry like me. His fur was fluffy and he had black eyes that were bigger than mine. He had a red ribbon around his neck instead of dog tags. He was too pretty to be a protector bear. At least, that's what I thought.

With a frown, Karen turned away and we went to the dining room where there were no new babies or bears hogging all the attention. We didn't like this pretender, this imposter, who thought he was going to take over MY job.

Karen squeezed me tight. "I love you, Alexander," she whispered in my ear. "You'll always be my special bear."

"He may look like Alexander, but he won't have the adventures this old bear has had, even if he lives as long as Alexander." Grampa Mike picked both Karen and me up and hugged us tight. "Alexander is a one of a kind bear. No one will ever replace him."

Thankfully they didn't name the imposter Alexander, too. Instead, they named him Bailey.

1976: Flying Fish

In 1976, I turned fifty-nine and the United States of America celebrated its 200th birthday. All the parties and such didn't matter too much to us because we were stationed in Germany. Karen and I were best pals. She was five years old. Whenever Wayne had some time off, he and Karen went fishing. I got to go a couple of times—that is, until the day I almost drown. That was also the day I caught my first and only fish.

It was late spring. It was almost warm enough not to wear coats, but I was real glad Karen had brought hers. I didn't need a coat. Bears carry their own with them.

I sat on a big boulder and watched as Karen and Wayne fished. They'd throw their lines out with hooks and bait on them, then sit and wait for a long time before reeling their lines back in. It looked pretty silly to me, but Wayne seemed to be having a good time. After about ten minutes, Karen got bored. She set her fishing pole aside and started to explore along the edge of the creek.

"Be careful, honey. Your mother will tan my hide if you catch a cold from falling in the water," Wayne said, throwing his line out again.

I was so busy watching Karen, I didn't see this big old ugly fish sneak up behind me. It was a real shock when I suddenly flew off my perch. That silly fish had jumped up and pushed me!

I somersaulted down the side of the rock and splashed in the creek. Thankfully, I was face up so I could see things. I saw Karen as I floated down the stream. Then I saw Wayne. I hoped someone would see me and pull me out of the water.

I'd scream for help, but I couldn't. After all, there are some things this bear just couldn't do. Swimming and calling for help were just two of them.

"Daddy, look! Alexander's swimming!" I heard Karen cry out.

Yeah, the bear's swimming and he's never had a lesson.

"Swimming? Oh, my. We'd better get him out of there," Wayne said, frowning at me. I wanted to tell him it wasn't my fault, it was that old fish that had shoved me.

I continued splashing down the creek, bouncing over rocks along the way. I thought I felt something bite my foot. Was the fish now trying to drown me? What did he think I was, lunch?

The water was cold. After all, it came down from the mountains where there was sometimes snow all summer long. The water started to soak through my fur. I was certain I was a goner. I was only a stuffed bear. I couldn't swim, and now there was something hanging on my foot and my insides were starting to get all wet.

The creek got bumpy again and I bounced some more, somehow each time bobbing to the surface again. Each time I came up for air, I saw Karen running along the edge of the creek. Wayne was right behind her, trying to figure out the best way to rescue me without getting soaked himself.

I wished he'd hurry up!

The creek settled down again because we'd reached the end of that set of rapids. Wayne boldly stepped into the creek and scooped me up with one hand. He tossed me onto the grassy bank next to where Karen stood. Then he climbed back out of the water.

"Boy, is that water cold!" He sat down next to me.

"Is Alexander going to be okay, Daddy?" Karen frowned as she picked me up and shook me. Water dripped off my fur in streams. Maybe I wouldn't drown after all. Thank goodness.

"He'll be fine, honey. And look here, he caught a fish!" Wayne unhooked the fish from my foot and held it up for his daughter to see.

"Bad fish!" Karen scolded.

"He's too little to keep. We'll have to come back next year and catch him again," Wayne said, before releasing it back into the creek.

"Next year, you catch it, Daddy. I don't think Alexander liked swimming." Karen wrapped me in her sweatshirt and carried me to the car. It was warm there so I waited there while they finished fishing.

When we got home that night, Karen dried me with her mother's hairdryer. She told her mother all about the only fish caught that day: the fish I'd caught without even trying.

1980: The Black Hole

If you've ever wondered if black holes are real, well, I'm here to tell you they are. A black hole is a big vacuum cleaner-like tear in the universe that sucks up everything in its path. And they don't just happen out in space. They're funny things, too. They come and go, and I'm not sure they're really even black. I think they're invisible, which makes them even more dangerous. Especially to little stuffed bears.

Joey and I met up with our first black hole in 1980. While the mysterious black hole was around, I wasn't sure I'd be able to protect anyone after Joey. After all, it's hard to keep family members safe if you've been sucked up into nothingness by a black hole.

Joey was forever losing things. Anything he laid down would disappear. Poof! One minute it would be there, the next it would be gone. I was afraid I'd be next. Karen, older by a handful of years, teased him that he had a black hole following him around. She was studying space in school and it sounded like she knew what she was talking about. The funny thing was, no one knew how right she was when she said it.

"Mom, have you seen my baseball glove?" Joey called from under his bed.

"No, I haven't. Is it in your room?" his mother asked.

"No. I've looked EVERYWHERE and it's gone!" Joey called back. "I think the black hole ate it."

In the Quigglebush household, the black hole was now blamed for everything that could not be found right away. I was just happy they didn't blame the bear.

"What black hole?" Joey's dad asked as he walked in from work.

"The black hole that's following me around! I've lost my favorite socks, my Dallas Cowboys' hat, and now my baseball glove."

"Well don't let Alexander fall into it. Your great grandmother would never forgive you," his dad said.

From then on, Joey carried me wherever he went in the house. When he left the yard, he carefully placed me on the kitchen table so I could keep an eye on the food. Of course, I thought that was boring since I don't eat food.

One day Joey and I saw the black hole in action. It was a scary thing. We were in the backyard playing fetch with Max, the family dog. They used Max's favorite toy, a grubby green tennis ball.

Joey threw the ball, and Max chased it and brought it back. Then they had to play Tug of War with the ball until Max let go and Joey could throw it again. The last time Joey threw the ball so hard it rolled under the bushes at the back of the yard. Max ran after it, but couldn't find it. Being a dog, he had a short attention span, so he decided instead to chase a squirrel that had dared to come into HIS yard.

Joey and I crawled under the bushes and looked for the tennis ball. His dad was cutting the front yard and would be back here soon. If the lawn mower ran over the tennis ball, it would chop it up into a zillion pieces. Then Max would be sad that his favoritist ball was gone. Max didn't like having to break in new tennis balls.

But the tennis ball wasn't under the bushes! We crawled all under those bushes and looked everywhere. The ball had vanished.

Hold me tight, I pleaded with Joey in silent bear talk. I don't want the black hole to suck me up too!

Finally, Joey gave up and we went back into the house and reported another sighting of the black hole.

In time, the black hole moved on to someone else. Everything that had disappeared during that scary week reappeared right where it had last been seen.

Weird, huh?

1983: The Stowaway

News got out that I was a terrific protector. The Quigglebushs sometimes loaned me out to friends who needed my special brand of protection. Which made for extra adventures for me. In 1983, I was loaned out to a friend of a friend of Karen's. Her dad was going on a real long trip. Karen said it was into space, but I didn't believe her. Not at first anyway. Not until I ended up there, too.

I was supposed to stay with Linda to keep her safe while her dad was gone, but she had other ideas. The day before her dad was supposed to leave, she hugged me all afternoon and evening. She cried a lot and that made me sad.

"I wish I was going with Dad. But since I can't go, at least you can keep him safe. That's what Karen tells me you're good at, keeping people safe. Dad's going to need protection in space."

I studied her and tried to tell her without words that I always kept my people safe. Even if they wanted to do things that weren't really safe, I did my job. Way late that night, we snuck out of her room and down the hall. Her dad's black briefcase was sitting by the front door, waiting for morning when he would leave to go on his trip.

"Take good care of my dad, Alexander. And protect the others, too," she whispered as she squeezed me real tight one last time. She opened the briefcase and stuffed me inside. Then she closed the top down on me and snapped it closed. I wanted to complain about being all smooshed flat, but there was no one to complain to. Besides, I don't talk, so I just kept the complaint to myself.

I couldn't hear anything after that, so I waited. I didn't know that we'd left the house and gone to the Space Center. Two men opened the case, examined me and the notebook underneath me. They approved us both to be placed aboard the Space Shuttle Challenger for its 7th mission into space.

"Who gets the bear?" One man asked as they finished packing the carts they'd brought on board.

"Don't know. Strap him in over there," the other man said.

Then they left and I waited some more. Soon the room shook really hard and the air felt funny around me.

"Hey, guys, looks like we've got a stowaway." A man took me from where I was tied in and showed me to other people. They all wore funny suits. A couple looked like snowmen the children built when we were in Alaska, but that's a whole other story.

"A stowaway? Alexander, how did you get here?" A familiar face at last. It was Linda's dad. I wanted to explain that it hadn't been my idea, but I'm sure he figured that out. I watched as we floated around the room. How did he do that? People weren't known for flying, but there we were, swimming through the air.

"Can't leave home without your teddy bear?" A lady's voice asked.

"This is Alexander T. Bear. He's been around for a lot of years and has traveled over most of the world. He's a bona fide hero, protecting generations of one family for more than sixty years. Linda must have hidden him in my briefcase."

"Now he can claim to be the first bear in space as well."

I was strapped to a wall again so I could protect the astronauts, but stay out of their way. Each time they talked to a funny screen in the living quarters, I was introduced as the official bear of STS-7.

It was an honor to be part of Space Shuttle Mission 7's trip into space. But I don't think I'll do it again. Been there, done that.

1990: The Camel

In 1990, Karen and I were working in the Saudi Arabian desert. Karen and Chip handed cases of water out of the back of the truck to a company of U.S. Army tank jockeys. This was our twentieth trip into the Saudi Arabian desert since arriving in the Middle East three months before. We each had a job to do. Karen drove. Chip complained. I protected them. This trip would be no different than the last nineteen. Those Iraqi soldiers didn't have a chance with Alexander T. Bear on duty.

From my perch on the truck's dashboard, I heard the Bedouins' language, but I didn't understand a word. They were probably hoping to trade with the convoy. It happened every time the group of trucks stopped. Suddenly groups of desert people appeared out of nowhere with camels, horses, goats, and all their belongings with them.

I faced the back of the truck so I couldn't see too much.

"Brrrumph."

The noise came from my left just before something clamped onto my arm.

Now I was used to Karen and Chip picking me up. They were gentle. They even hugged me tight when homesickness was especially hard to live with. After all, we were on the other side of the world from our families.

No one had ever grabbed me up by one arm before. Not even when I was a new teddy bear, years and years before. I would have yelled for Karen, but everyone knows teddy bears can't talk. But I could listen and comfort and protect Karen and her friends.

I floated out the window of the truck, dangling by my shoulder a long, long way up from the sand and black road. I couldn't even see who was carrying me.

"Karen, that camel has that furry friend of yours," a deep voice shouted from behind me.

Karen raced toward us and grabbed me by my other arm and both legs. I wished I didn't have to see Karen struggle with my kidnapper. It wasn't a pretty sight.

"Let go of him, you idiot camel!" Karen demanded. Releasing my legs, she smacked my kidnapper, then pulled me free. I felt something tear in my shoulder.

"Oh, Alexander, your shoulder!" She cried as she hugged me close. "Chip, get the first aid kit. We have to patch Alexander up before all his stuffing bleeds out."

I wondered if a stuffed bear could die from losing his stuffing. No, Karen would fix me up. She and her father, and the rest of her family had taken care of me just as I'd taken care of them for years and years and years.

That night in our tent between the two Saudi Arabian airports, Karen laid me on her bunk. She brushed away her tears as she unwrapped the white bandage from my shoulder.

"I don't know what got into that camel. Normally they stay away from the trucks. I guess you'll have to stay here from now on. It's too dangerous in the truck. I just hope you keep protecting me, even though you're not with me."

She picked up her needle and thread, and stitched my torn shoulder seam back together. The green thread and big stitches closed the hole, but were ugly against my brown wool fur.

"Well, my friend, I guess you'll just have to wear a bandage for a while, at least until we can take proper care of that wound."

Karen bandaged my shoulder with a white dressing pad and some tape. She was careful to keep the chain that held my silver dog tag free from the bandage. The tag read:

Alexander T. Bear

Quigglebush Family Hero

Veteran of many trips abroad

"There. Now you look like the hero we all know you are."

1999: The Rescue

In the spring of 1999, Karen and I flew Pedro rescue helicopters for the National Guard. Our unit was assigned to eastern North Carolina, where people needed to be rescued from the worst flooding in the state's history.

"Hey, Bearman, you ready to keep us superheroes safe?" Carlos Menendez, the crew chief, said as he squeezed my arm, then rubbed one finger up and down my belly just as he did before every flight.

I stared at him without replying. I wanted to tell him, again, that my name was Alexander, NOT Bearman.

"His name is Alexander, or if you prefer, 'Oh Great and Powerful Mr. Bear, Protector of the Quigglebush family and their Chosen Friends,'" Karen joked as she strapped herself into her seat. "We may take you off that list if you're not careful."

The copilot climbed into his seat and prepared to take off. A family was trapped on the roof of their house about twenty miles from town.

"Forgive me, Oh Great and Powerful Good Luck Bear. Whatever magic you're working, please keep it up." Carlos said, as he returned to the belly of the helicopter to prepare for the mission.

Karen reached up to where I was strapped into my special place by her shoulder. She rubbed my foot, then squeezed my leg. "Okay, old man, let's go rescue somebody."

She sounded distracted. Was she missing her husband, Shane? Or was it her son, Paul, who was on her mind? I know I missed my warm, dry place on the bookcase in the living room. Here we were, wet and cold and busy, busy, busy. But saving people was our job, and we were good at that job. We'd even won awards for how well we performed as a team.

I wished I could hug Karen just then, but I was just a small bear. When we were alone, she hugged me lots. Just like all the Quigglebushs before her had done when they were sad or lonely or scared.

In minutes, we were flying over eastern North Carolina. Only there wasn't any ground down below us. Everything was covered with brown water. Only treetops and roofs of some buildings could be seen above all the water.

"There," Tim, the copilot, pointed toward a house that had a group of people standing on the roof.

"Okay, Carlos, we're here," Karen announced into her headphone.

The helicopter hovered as low over the roof as Karen could hold it without blowing the people off into the water. Carlos and the new guy lifted the people from the roof one at a time using a seat attached to a rope like a swing.

The littlest boy was only about three and he wasn't happy. He screamed so loud that I could hear him over the sound of the engine. It was very distracting.

"Carlos, what's wrong?" Karen asked, then listened for a moment. "Yeah, he might help. Come get him."

A moment later, Carlos undid my straps and we moved to the back of the helicopter.

"Please, Alexander, work your teddy bear magic and calm this kid down," Carlos ordered as we moved to the seat beside the boy and his mother.

Carlos buckled himself into his seat before handing me to the source of all the noise. "Hey, kiddo, this is my friend, Alexander. Can you hold onto him until we land?"

I stared at the child who'd stopped crying long enough to study me. The poor kid was soaked to the skin. I guess he wasn't a bear person. He held me in both hands, raised me over his head and threw me as hard as he could. He screamed at Carlos, "I don't want Bear. I want JoJo."

"No! Alexander!" Carlos screeched. He reached out to catch me as I flew past him, but he was strapped in and couldn't reach me in time.

I somersaulted once more and flew out the open door of the helicopter. As the cold air ruffled my fur, I started to worry about Karen, Carlos, and the rest of the crew. What would they do without Alexander, their good luck bear?

So there I was without even a parachute to slow me down. I hoped Karen would be waiting on the ground to catch me.

I was surprised that I didn't end up in the river when I landed. I bounced once on a road, then landed with my left foot in a mud puddle. All I could see was the road. Someone was talking, but I couldn't understand the words for a moment. "Brutus, fetch. Bring back the bird that helicopter hit."

I wanted to tell him that I wasn't a bird, I was a bear. And I was right here laying half in this mud puddle. I wanted to ask someone to pick me up and wipe off my nose. But I couldn't since everyone knows teddy bears don't talk.

A moment later, somebody nudged me, then picked me up. I felt teeth around my middle, but it wasn't like when the camel tried to eat me when we were in the Gulf. Whoever held me now was very careful not to hold me too tight.

"Brutus, return. Bring me the bird," the man ordered.

In response, we started moving fast, way faster than I think I've ever moved before. Then I was flying again. This time I landed on top of a wet, mud-spattered boot.

"Good dog, Brutus."

Someone picked me up. Then I looked into a face, but it wasn't Karen. It was a man with dark skin I'd never seen before.

"It's a teddy bear, Daddy," a little voice said. "Can I have it?"

"Just a minute, Honey." The man studied me, then read the paper tag Karen had tied around my neck when we'd arrived in North Carolina. It had her contact information, just in case we got separated. "Alexander T. Bear, eh? Well, Mr. Bear, I guess you're coming with us to higher ground. When we get to town, we'll see if we can find the person who lost you. You're in charge of Mr. Bear until we find his owner, Honey. Okay?"

"Yes, Daddy."

Honey was young and she looked scared. She stared at me and I stared back at her for a long time. This girl and her family were my responsibility until we could find Karen.

"Okay, Mr. Bear, let's go." Honey tucked me inside her yellow rain slicker. Both our heads stuck out of the neck hole. We followed her father and the rest of her family through the fields and woods until we came to the floodwaters.

"Daddy?" Honey took his hand and together we all studied the waters that rushed past. The road we'd been following disappeared into the water. I couldn't see where the other side of the water was.

We turned around and hiked back to the field. More people joined us until there were almost a dozen people standing in a circle. Honey's dad pulled out a cell phone and made a call. Then we waited.

About twenty minutes later, two helicopters appeared over the treetops and landed.

Honey's dad and the men from the helicopter made sure everyone else was safe on one helicopter or the other before lifting Honey and me into one. We settled into the middle seat next to a man in a green uniform. She unbuttoned her coat, then hugged me tight. "We'll find your people, Alexander," she said.

"Who's your friend?" the soldier said, leaning over to check me out.

Honey held me out so I could see Carlos's surprised face. "Somebody lost their teddy bear. His name is Alexander. Our dog, Brutus, rescued him, and I'm gonna take care of him until I find his person named Quigglebush."

"Holy cats! It is Alexander. We thought you were gone for good!" Carlos jumped up then leaned into the cockpit. "Guess who we just picked up!"

When we landed, Honey hugged me tight before handing me over to Karen. Karen hugged me tight as well. From then on, we carried other stuffed animals to share with the kids we rescued. I stayed in the cockpit where it was safe.

1999: New Clothes

I am a well-loved bear. After eighty-three years of living with the Quigglebushs, I've protected my family and had a lot of adventures. But time and love can wear a bear out.

I was losing my fur. But then I wasn't the only one. Sam, and Mike's son, Wayne, were both showing more skin than fur on their heads, too.

The end of the year was coming, and the New Year would start a whole new century. The new millennium, people called it. Some were worried about the world coming to an end. I was worried about my fur.

Cousins Victoria and Mara were dressing the new dolls they'd gotten for Christmas a few days before. I looked on from my latest home on the shelf over the fireplace. Karen called the shelf a mantle. I didn't care what it was called as long as it was warm and dry.

"You know," Mara said, looking up at me, "Alex needs some clothes. He must be cold sitting there with nothing on but his dog tags."

Victoria looked at me, then at all the clothes lying on the floor between them. "Let's dress up Alexander," she said.

Let's not, I thought. There was no way this bear would wear a dress. I am, after all, a boy.

Leave me alone. I have fur. I don't need clothes.

"That's a great idea!" Mara stood up and reached for me. Thankfully the shelf was high and she was short.

"Mom," she called into the dining room where the adults were talking.

"Yes?" Josh came out to see what the fuss was about.

"You're not Mom. You're Dad," Victoria giggled.

"Yeah, Uncle Josh, you're a dad," Mara said, then turned to Victoria. "But at least he's tall."

"Yeah, he can do it, I guess," Victoria agreed after thinking a moment.

"What am I tall enough to do?" Josh asked.

"Could you please hand Alexander down from his shelf?" Victoria asked in her most polite voice.

Josh looked from Victoria to Mara, then to me. "I don't know. Alexander is getting to be an old man. He's not up to much wrestling anymore."

Ha, I said to myself, bring it on. I've been around the world, up in space and am holding together better than any other eighty-three-year-old I know. A little playtime with these two won't do me any harm.

The girls giggled. "We don't want to wrestle with him, Daddy. We want to dress him up. He looks cold," Victoria said.

"Dress him up, huh? I suppose it's okay." Josh picked me up off my shelf and handed me to Mara.

"Thanks, Uncle Josh," Mara hugged me close.

If I could have, I would have smiled just then. Being hugged is one of my most favorite things.

"So, how should we dress him?" Mara asked, as they sorted through their piles of doll clothes.

"Well, he's not a girl, so we can't put him in a dress. Maybe a suit?" Victoria held up a purple jacket that had ruffles on it.

No way, I protested silently.

"No. Alexander is a working bear. And purple is not his color," Mara said.

Thank you, Mara. You are now my favorite Quigglebush.

"How about overalls?" Victoria held up her second choice. It was a pair of blue and white pants that had funny straps on them.

"How about Army clothes for the family's patriot bear," someone said from across the room.

The little girls squealed that high screeching sound that only they can make.

"Aunt Karen, you scared us!" the cousins said together.

"Sorry girls. I heard you were going to dress Alexander and thought you might want to try this on him." Karen handed Victoria a small paper bag. "I'm not sure they'll fit, but you can try."

Victoria opened the bag, poured the clothes out onto the floor and giggled some more. While Mara held me, Victoria wrestled the pants and shirt on me.

I didn't want to wear clothes, but at least these didn't choke me.

"They fit perfectly," Mara said.

She carried me to a mirror and let me see myself.

"Look Alexander. Now you are a real patriot bear. This army suit is perfect."

"Now you won't be cold and people won't see that you're losing your fur," Victoria said as she rubbed my head.

Once the girls finished buttoning and adjusting my new clothes, making sure I looked perfect, they carried me into the dining room. We showed my new and improved self to the rest of the family.

And that is how I came to be a clothes-wearing bear.

The End…for now

.

Alexander is currently retired and living in New Bern, North Carolina, waiting for the next time he'll be needed in his role as Protector Bear.

Susan Eileen Walker lives in a cabin in the woods, with her dog, Honey, also known as The Princess Fuzzybutt, who protects her from squirrels, rabbits, deer, and any other oddities they come across during their daily walks.

Made in the USA
Middletown, DE
15 March 2023

26829069R00046